4th of July Jokes For Kids

Maureen Kalember

What kind of tea did the American colonists want?
Liberty!

Who was the biggest jokester in George Washington's army?
Laughayette!

Why did Benjamin Franklin fly his kite in a storm?

He didn't want anyone to steal his thunder!

What cat said, "The British are coming! The British are coming!"?

Paw Revere.

What did the visitor say as she left the Statue of Liberty?

"Keep in torch!"

Why was King George a foot tall?

Because he was a ruler.

Where can a pig see the statue of liberty?
New Pork City!

Why did George Washington have trouble sleeping?
Because he couldn't lie!

What happened as a result of the Stamp Act?
The Americans licked the British!

Who is mentioned in the Star- Spangled Banner?
Jose Kanusee.

How do you great
someone on
Independence Day?
"May the fourth be with
you!"

What happens when fog
lifts in southern
California?
UCLA!

What do you call doing 2,000 pounds of laundry?
Washing-ton!

Why did the beauty queen not want to leave the colonies?
She said she would Miss America.

Why does the Statue of Liberty stand in New York Harbor?
Because she can't sit down!

What was Thomas Jefferson's favorite dessert?
Monti Jello!

What famous pig signed the Declaration of Independence?
John Hamcock!

What march would you play at a jungle parade?
"Tarzan Stripes Forever"!

What is the capital of Alaska?
Oh, Juneau this one!

Why did the British soldiers wear red coat?
So they could hide in the tomatoes.

What is Uncle Sam's favorite snack?
Fire crackers!

What do you call an American drawing?
A Yankee doodle!

What do you call someone from Detroit who talks a lot?
A Motor City mouth!

What's red, white, blue, and green?
A patriotic pickle.

Why did the British cross the Atlantic?
To get to the other tide!

Did you hear the one about the Libery Bell?
It cracked me up!

Why can't a woman living in the U.S. be buried in England?
Because she's still alive!

What was General Washington's favorite tree?
The infantry!

Where to pencils come from?
Pennsylvania!

What has four legs, a shiny nose, and fought for England?
Rudolph the Redcoat Reindeer!

What is the smartest state?

Alabama, it has four A's and one B!

What would you call the USA if everyone lived in their cars?

An incarnation!

Why was the barbecue man happy?
He finally found the grill of his dreams.

What kind of music did the Pilgrims like?
Plymouth Rock!

What did they call a dentist in the Continental Army?
A drill sergeant.

In what U.S. state can you find tiny drinks?
Mini-soda!

What would you get if you crossed the first U.S. president with an animated character?
George Washingtoon!

What do you call a fake patriot?
Uncle Sham.

What did Delaware?
Her New Jersey!

What did the colonists wear to the Boston Tea Party?
Tea-shirts.

What was the craziest battle of the Revolutionary War?
The Battle of Bonkers Hill.

What do you get if you cross a patriot with a small curly-haired dog?
Yankee Poodle.

Why did the volleyball player join the Continental Army?
To serve our country.

When is the best month to have a 4th of July parade?
March!

Why does the Mississippi river see so well?
Because it has 4 eyes!

What did Tennessee?
The same thing as Arkansas.

What do you eat on July 5th?

Independence Day-Old-Pizza!

Which colonists told the most jokes?

Punsylvanians!

What do you call the hippie's wife? Mississippi!

What was a patriot's favorite food during the Revolutionary War?
Chicken Catch-a-Tory!

What do you call a dinosaur that eats fireworks?
A dino-mite!

What do you call George Washington's false teeth?
Presidentures!

Where do you dance in California?
San Frandisco!

What's the happiest state in the union?
Merry-land!

How is George Washington like the New England Patriots?
They both like to be ahead in quarters.

Where was the Declaration of Independence signed?
At the bottom.

What protest by a group of dogs occurred in 1772?

The Boston Flea Party!

Which famous person do you get when you make a wreath out of $100 bills?

Aretha Franklin!

What would you get if you crossed the American national bird with Snoopy?
A bald beagle!

Where does a parade of horses go on the Fourth of July?
Mane Street.

What did Polly the parrot want for the 4th of July?

A fire cracker!

How did George Washington speak to his army?

In general terms!

What are the last two words of The Star-Spangled Banner?
Play ball!

How was the at the Fourth of July picnic?
The hot dogs were bad, but the brats were the wurst!

What did the fuse say to the firecracker?
Lets get together and pop it like it's hot!

What did King George think of the American colonists?
He thought they were revolting!

How come there are no Knock Knock jokes about America?
Because freedom rings!

Where do the pianists go for vacation?
The Florida Keys!

Who wrote, "Oh say, can you see?"'
An eye doctor!

Knock, knock!
Who's there?
Hawaii!
Hawaii Who?
I'm fine, Hawaii you?

What U.S. state is round on the ends and high in the middle?
Ohio!

What is the capital of Washington?
W!

What did you get if you ran over a Continental Army officer with a steam roller?
A flat major.

What quacks, has webbed feet, and betrays his country?
Beneduck Arnold!

What would you get if you crossed Washington's home with nasty insects?
Mt. Vermin!

What did the patriot put on his dry skin?
Revo-lotion!

What did the Revolutionary War pigeon say at the meeting?
"Coup, coup!"

Was General Washington a handsome man?
Yes, he was George-eous!!

Why did Paul Revere ride his horse from Boston to Lexington?
Because the horse was too heavy to carry!

What would you get if you crossed George Washington with cattle feed?
The Fodder of Our Country!

What would you call the USA if everyone had a pink car?
A pink carnation!

What has feathers, webbed feet, and certain inalienable rights?
The Ducklaration of Independence.

What's red, white, blue and green?
A seasick Uncle Sam.

Why were the first Americans like ants?
They lived in colonies!

What did one American flag say to the other flag?
Nothing it just waved.

Where did George Washington keep his armies?
In his sleevies!

What was the most popular dance in 1776?
Indepen-dance!

What rock group has four guys who don't sing?
Mount Rushmore!

Why did the Pilgrims want to sail to America in the spring?

Because April showers bring Mayflowers.

Where did George Washington buy his hatchet?

At the chopping mall.

Knock, Knock.
Who's there?
Alaska!
Alaska who?
Alaska later right now
I'm busy!

What did one firecracker
say to the other
firecracker?
"My pop's bigger than
your pop."

What are the Great Plains?
The 747, Concorde and F-16!

What's the difference between a duck and George Washington?
One has a bill on his face, and the other has his face on a bill!

Why wouldn't Washing leave the kitchen?
He kept going through his cabinet.

What do you get if you cross the first signer of the Declaration of Independence with a rooster?
John Hancock-a-doodle-doo.

What's red, white and blue?
A sad candy cane!

What U.S. state is best at producing cheese?
Swiss-consin!

What do you call a city without mini apples? Mini-apple-less.

What is in the center of America?
The letter R!

Made in the USA
San Bernardino, CA
12 June 2020